WITHDRAWN

Monday
Is
One Day

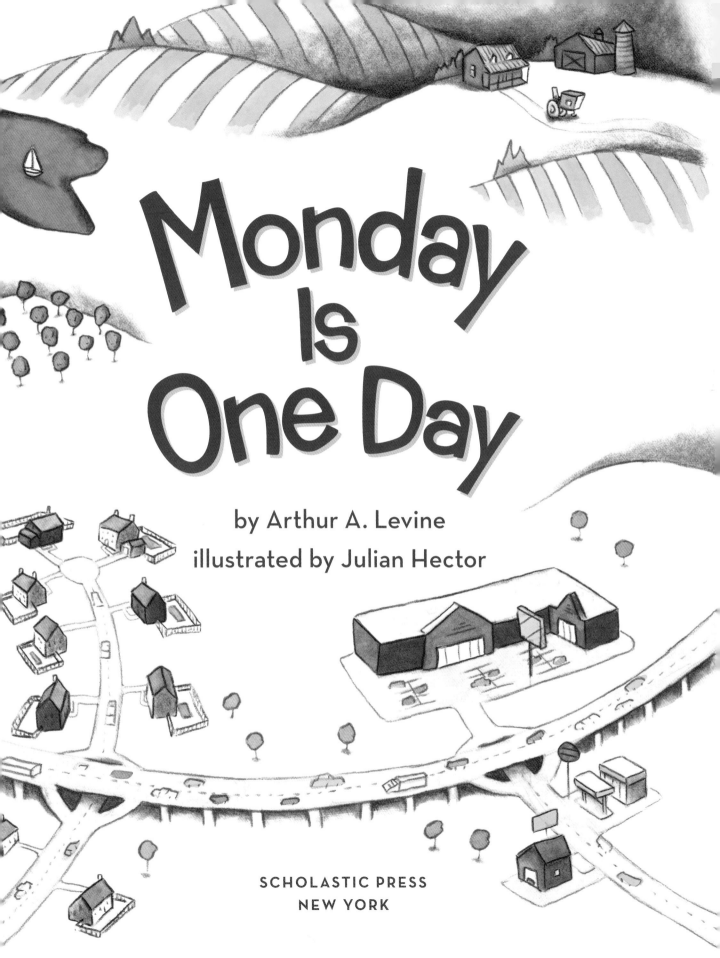

Monday Is One Day

by Arthur A. Levine

illustrated by Julian Hector

SCHOLASTIC PRESS
NEW YORK

Library of Congress Cataloging-in-Publication Data

Levine, Arthur A., 1962-
Monday is one day / by Arthur A. Levine ; illustrated by Julian Hector. -- 1st ed.
p. cm.
Summary: A rhyming countdown of the days of the week as a father and
child find ways to spend time together while waiting for the weekend.
ISBN 978-0-439-78924-0
[1. Stories in rhyme. 2. Days--Fiction. 3. Week--Fiction.
4. Parent and child--Fiction. 5. Counting--Fiction.]
I. Hector, Julian, ill. II. Title.
PZ8.3.L577Mo 2011
[E]--dc22
2009011575

10 9 8 7 6 5 4 3 2 1   11 12 13 14 15
Printed in Singapore 46
First edition, April 2011
Book design by Elizabeth B. Parisi and Christopher Stengel

For my only Max Emilio, from whom
my heart is never parted. — A. L.

To Namrata Tripathi. — J. H.

The hardest part of going to
work is being apart from you.

Let's count the days till we're both at home with a special thing to do.

Monday is one day:
One safe snuggly cuddle.

Tuesday's blue shoes day:
Two stomps in a puddle.

Wednesday's halfway day:
Three raspberries on the nose.

Thursday is Grrrrr Day!
Four T. Rex growls before I go.

Friday's last-tie day:
Can you help me pick the one?

Saturday, we're on our way!
Let's race in the sun.

And Sunday's our fun day:
A kiss and a cuddle,
A dance in a puddle,
A dinosaur huddle,
A sweet family muddle!

Monday through Sunday,
the whole week through,
each day I count the ways
I love to be with you!